47

MONSTERS

First published 1979 by Victor Gollancz Ltd

This edition published 2013 by Walker Books Ltd
87 Vauxhall Walk, London SE11 5HJ

2 4 6 8 10 9 7 5 3 1

This book has been typeset in Adobe Garamond

Printed in China

British Library Cataloguing in Publication Data:
a catalogue record for this book is available from the British Library

ISBN 978-1-4063-4953-5

www.walker.co.uk

MONSTERS

Russell Hoban & Quentin Blake

WALKER BOOKS
AND SUBSIDIARIES
LONDON · BOSTON · SYDNEY · AUCKLAND

John liked to draw monsters.

He drew monsters that looked like puddings with teeth, he drew monsters that had hundreds of eyes and odd numbers of ears, he drew scaly monsters, furry monsters, vegetable and mineral monsters, and unheard-of monsters that were so monstrous they had to be invisible so they wouldn't scare themselves to death.

He drew red, yellow, blue, green and purple monsters and he drew spotted monsters and monsters that were all blotchy with different colours.

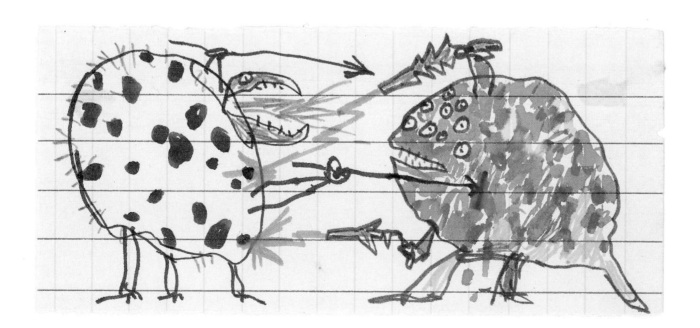

All John's monsters were violent. They fought with passing strangers and random spacecraft and they fought with one another, and if they found themselves alone they made threatening noises to themselves while waiting for somebody ugly to turn up.

"*GNGGHHHH!*" they said, "*NNARRRGH!*" and "*XURRRVVV!*"

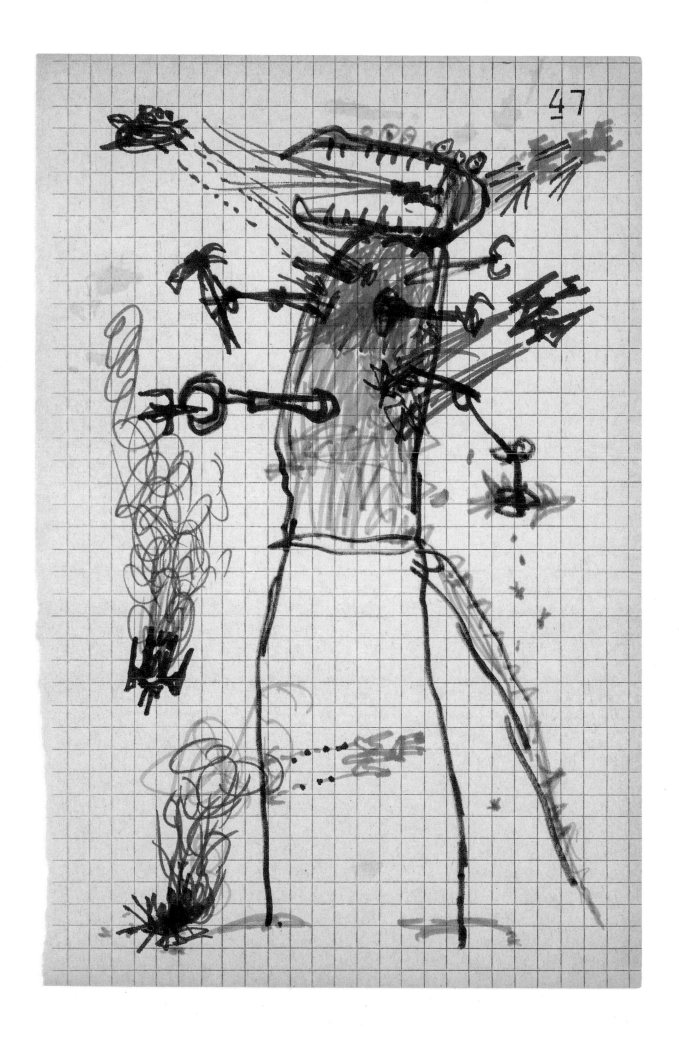

John's monsters breathed smoke and fire and they used their teeth and their claws when they fought.

They also used guided missiles, lasers, bows and arrows, spears, clubs and rocks.

John was drawing a battle between an army of red monsters wielding hammers and an army of green monsters with tongs when his mother looked over his shoulder. "Don't you ever get tired of drawing monsters?" she said.

"Not really," said John. "Monsters are my favourite thing to draw."

"Still," said Mum, "there are so many other nice things to draw. There are houses and trees and birds and animals."

"Monsters are animals," said John.

"I mean real animals like dogs and cats," said Mum, "or even lions and tigers if you like."

"Monsters are real," said John.

"Have you ever seen one?" said Mum.

"I've seen them on TV," said John.

"Yes," said Mum, "but have you ever seen one just walking around?"

"Not yet," said John.

"Everything all right at school?" said Dad. "Getting on with the other boys and all that?"

"Yes," said John.

"And your teachers," said Mum, "what about them?"

"They're all right," said John.

"Any trouble with any of your subjects?" said Dad. "I used to have a terrible time with maths and history."

"I'm not having any trouble with anything," said John. "Have you got any really big pieces of paper?"

"I've got some big sheets of brown wrapping paper," said Mum. She gave them to John.

"Thank you," said John. He took the wrapping paper and his felt-tip pens up to his room.

When Mum and Dad came up to kiss John goodnight they saw that he'd done a drawing that filled up a whole sheet of wrapping paper.

"What is it?" said Dad.

"It's the tip of a tail," said John.

"Very spiky," said Mum. "Where's the rest of whatever it is?"

"Coming," said John.

"Must be pretty big," said Dad.

"I guess so," said John.

"What will it be?" said Mum.

"I don't know," said John. "I haven't seen the other end of it yet."

When John was asleep Dad said to Mum, "That drawing doesn't seem quite the same as John's other drawings."

"No," said Mum, "it doesn't. It seems somehow more serious than the others."

"It does," said Dad, "and if just the tip of the tail filled up that big piece of paper the whole thing must be very serious indeed."

The next day Mum and Dad went to see John's art teacher, Mr Splodge. "What do you think of John's drawings?" said Dad.

"First rate," said Mr Splodge. "His monsters are in a class by themselves."

Mum showed him the drawing on the brown paper. "What do you think of this one?" she said.

"This tail is very well done," said Mr Splodge. "It almost jumps right off the paper at you, doesn't it."

"John says the rest of it is coming," said Dad.

"Should be quite impressive," said Mr Splodge.

"You're not bothered about it?" said Dad.

"Why should I be bothered?" said Mr Splodge.

"Well, it's such a serious-looking tail," said Dad, "and whatever's on the other end of it is going to be so very big."

"I shouldn't worry about it if I were you," said Mr Splodge. "Boys are naturally a little monstrous."

The next morning Mum and Dad found another drawing on John's desk. "I think we ought to talk to Dr Plunger," said Dad. So they went to Dr Plunger's office and showed him the two drawings.

"This could be something very big," said Dr Plunger.

"That's what we thought," said Mum.

"Are you worried about it?" said Dr Plunger.

"Yes, we are," said Dad.

Dr Plunger wrote out a prescription. "Take the tablets as directed," he said, "and if the drawings continue let me see the next one."

The next day Mum and Dad brought in a third drawing.

"Dear me," said Dr Plunger. "Perhaps I'd better have a chat with John."

When Mum and Dad brought John in for a chat,
Dr Plunger said, "Tell me about these drawings, John."

"I haven't got a piece of paper that's big enough," said
John. "That's why I have to do it this way."

"Looks as if it's going to be something really big,"
said Dr Plunger.

"I can't say till I've seen the whole thing," said John.

"If I give you some felt-tip pens and some brown wrapping paper," said Dr Plunger, "do you think you could finish it for me?"

"Are you sure you want me to?" said John.

"Yes, indeed," said Dr Plunger.

"All right," said John. When Dr Plunger gave him the paper and the pens he began to draw very fast, moving from one sheet of brown paper to the next.

In the waiting room Mum and Dad heard a noise like two
or three heavy-metal rock bands all playing at once. There wasn't
a lot of music to it, it was mostly thumping and bumping and
crashing around.

After a while it stopped and they heard John say, "See you."
Then he came out of Dr Plunger's office with a big smile
on his face.

"Quite a lively time you seemed to be having in there,"
said Dad.

"You look very relaxed," said Mum.

"I feel pretty good, actually," said John.

"Did I hear you say you'd be seeing him again?" said Mum.

"Who?" said John.

"Dr Plunger," said Mum.

"I don't think so," said John.

"Get everything worked out, did you?" said Dad.

"Oh yes," said John, "everything worked out."

"No more monster drawings?" said Mum.

"Drawings?" said John as the door behind him slowly opened.

"Who needs drawings?"

The End